12 11 10 9 8 7 6 5 4 3 2   2 3 4 5 6 7/0

Book design: Cezanne Studio

Printed in the U.S.A.
First printing, November 2002

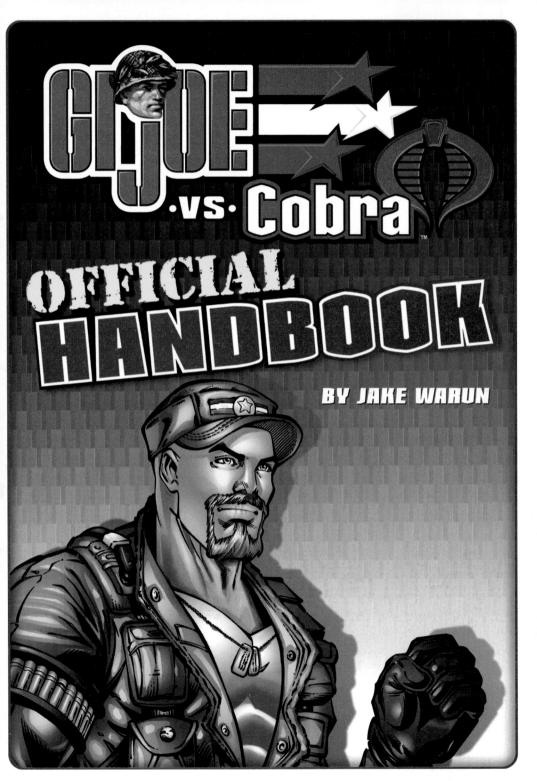

G.I. JOE vs. Cobra

OFFICIAL HANDBOOK

BY JAKE WARUN

SCHOLASTIC INC.
New York   Toronto   London   Auckland   Sydney
Mexico City   New Delhi   Hong Kong   Buenos Aires

G.I. JOE is a highly secret, special mission force formed to fight the evils of the COBRA organization. Reporting directly to the President of the United States, the G.I. JOE team has the top resources of the government available to them.

Formed by GENERAL TOMAHAWK and led by DUKE, the G.I. JOE team recruits only the best of the best from all divisions of the U.S. military: Navy SEALs, Army Rangers, Delta Force, Green Berets. Only those who pass the grueling physical, mental, and ethical tests will be selected to join the team!

Intent on taking over the world, COBRA has established a secret network of soldiers and spies, with bases around the world. Led by COBRA COMMANDER, the COBRA organization is disguised as a legitimate business dealing with real estate, household products, and technology services.

COBRA is evil to the core, and will stop at nothing. Now it is hatching a whole new brand of evil, with new schemes to bring down the governments of the free world. But the G.I. JOE team is committed to the cause of freedom for all people, and will stop at nothing to defeat COBRA. That's why each G.I. JOE soldier is a REAL AMERICAN HERO! G.I. JOE vs. COBRA — it's a battle for freedom!

Now, learn all about your favorite G.I. JOE heroes and COBRA agents by reading their secret files. Plus, you can read about all the new G.I. JOE and COBRA attack vehicles.

Everything you ever wanted to know about G.I. JOE and COBRA is finally here! **YO JOE!**

SNAKE EYES

CODE NAME: SNAKE EYES
COMMANDO
FILE NAME: CLASSIFIED
PRIMARY MILITARY SPECIALTY: INFANTRY
SECONDARY MILITARY SPECIALTY:
HAND-TO-HAND COMBAT INSTRUCTOR
BIRTHPLACE: CLASSIFIED   GRADE: E7
HEIGHT: 5'11"   WEIGHT: 175 lb
SN: CLASSIFIED

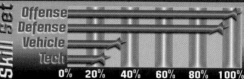

Skill Set

	0%	20%	40%	60%	80%	100%
Offense						
Defense						
Vehicle						
Tech						

"The ability to move quickly and silently is my greatest weapon."

SNAKE EYES learned his top combat skills in missions around the globe. A tragic helicopter mission took away his voice and scarred his face. That's why he never removes his mask. SNAKE EYES is an expert in all disciplines of martial arts and silent weapons. He studied mystical martial arts with the Arashikage clan, which is also the family of master ninja STORM SHADOW. Now that STORM SHADOW is part of the evil COBRA organization, there is no escape from a final battle between two of the world's greatest martial arts fighters.

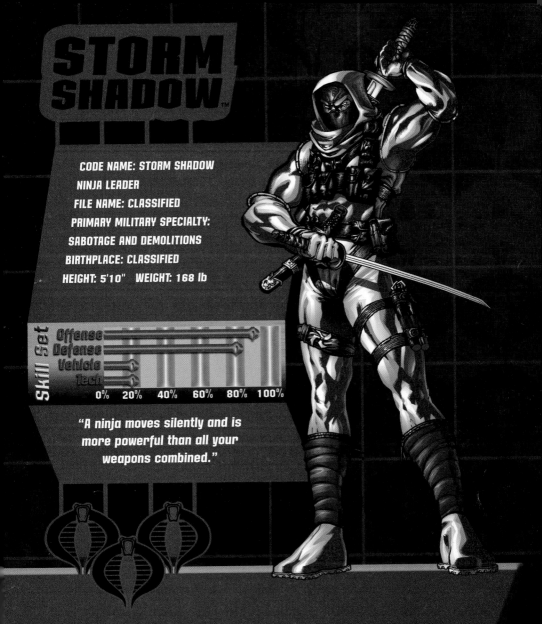

STORM SHADOW

CODE NAME: STORM SHADOW
NINJA LEADER
FILE NAME: CLASSIFIED
PRIMARY MILITARY SPECIALTY:
SABOTAGE AND DEMOLITIONS
BIRTHPLACE: CLASSIFIED
HEIGHT: 5'10"   **WEIGHT:** 168 lb

Skill Set

	0%	20%	40%	60%	80%	100%
Offense						
Defense						
Vehicle						
Tech						

*"A ninja moves silently and is
more powerful than all your
weapons combined."*

STORM SHADOW grew up in the Arashikage clan of ninjas.
During his training, his sword brother was SNAKE EYES, the
commando and martial arts master on the G.I. JOE team.
After a COBRA agent killed the uncle of STORM SHADOW,
he went undercover within COBRA to find the assassin.
When the killer was revealed, STORM SHADOW joined
the G.I. JOE team to get revenge. But now STORM
SHADOW is back with COBRA. And his anger is clear
when he meets SNAKE EYES. The battle between the
ninja masters will be legendary.

GUNG-HO

CODE NAME: GUNG-HO
MARINE RECON COMMANDER
FILE NAME: LAFITTE, ETTIENE R.
PRIMARY MILITARY SPECIALTY: RECONNAISSANCE
SECONDARY MILITARY SPECIALTY: HEAVY WEAPONS
BIRTHPLACE: FER-DE-LANCE, LOUISIANA
GRADE: E7 (SERGEANT)
HEIGHT: 6'0" WEIGHT: 200 lb
SN: 656-2456-ER89

Skill Set			
Offense			
Defense			
Vehicle			
Tech			

0%   20%   40%   60%   80%   100%

"I like things hot: my food and my missions! Send me where it's meanest—that's why I'm a Marine!"

GUNG-HO grew up in the Louisiana swamps. He's at home in brown water environments and thrives on all the heat, humidity, bugs, and alligators. He graduated top of his class from boot camp at Parris Island, then went on to join the G.I. JOE team. In Operation Swampfire, GUNG-HO destroyed a major advanced-technology weapons plant owned by DESTRO. The operation cost DESTRO a lot of money and set his organization back for years — and made GUNG-HO a sworn enemy of DESTRO.

DESTRO

CODE NAME: DESTRO
FILE NAME: DESTRO, JAMES MCCULLEN
PRIMARY MILITARY SPECIALTY: WEAPONS MANUFACTURER
SECONDARY MILITARY SPECIALTY: THIEF
BIRTHPLACE: CALLENDER, SCOTLAND
HEIGHT: 6'2"   WEIGHT: 228 lb

Skill Set

Offense
Defense
Vehicle
Tech

0%   20%   40%   60%   80%   100%

"Some people call me corrupt. To me, I'm just a businessman supplying what people want."

The DESTRO family builds and supplies weapons to any side that can meet their price. The latest leader of the DESTRO clan is very dangerous. He often steals secrets from governments around the world. Then his corporation sells the secrets and makes big profits. DESTRO wears a silver warrior mask (a family tradition) when in battle. Recently, his North American operations were damaged by GUNG-HO, causing DESTRO to lose millions of dollars. Now, DESTRO is out for revenge against GUNG-HO and the G.I. JOE team.

HEAVY DUTY

CODE NAME: HEAVY DUTY
HEAVY ORDNANCE SPECIALIST
FILE NAME: MORRIS, LAMONT
PRIMARY MILITARY SPECIALTY: HEAVY ANTI-ARMOR
WEAPONS SPECIALIST
SECONDARY MILITARY SPECIALTY:
INDIRECT FIRE INFANTRYMAN
BIRTHPLACE: CHICAGO, ILLINOIS
GRADE: E5   HEIGHT: 6'8"   WEIGHT: 280 lb
SN: 807-0246-LM65

Skill Set	0%	20%	40%	60%	80%	100%
Offense						
Defense						
Vehicle						
Tech						

"The rich sounds of violins
and anti-tank missiles are both
music to my ears."

HEAVY DUTY is a big city guy with heart and soul. And he loves going up against huge COBRA forces. He's an expert in heavy artillery and has been known to create his own weapons when nothing else is exactly what he needs. In Operation China Shop, he came up against COBRA C.L.A.W.S. for the first time. The two fought each other with matching SRCDs (Short-Range Cannon Destroyers) until the COBRA C.L.A.W.S. were forced to retreat. But HEAVY DUTY knows that he will be facing more COBRA C.L.A.W.S. and their heavy artillery again.

COBRA C.L.A.W.S.™

CODE NAME: COBRA C.L.A.W.S. (COMBAT LIGHT ARMORED WEAPONS SPECIALIST)

HEAVY WEAPONS TROOPER

AVERAGE HEIGHT: 5'10"

AVERAGE WEIGHT: 180 lb

Skill Set						
Offense						
Defense						
Vehicle						
Tech						
	0%	20%	40%	60%	80%	100%

"Our weapons are the best—we can squeeze the enemy into a corner, no matter how much muscle they've got."

COBRA C.L.A.W.S. are the elite troops of COBRA. These lightly armored heavy weapons specialists can take a lot of punishment and dish out even more. With new lightweight, ionized fiber armor (developed from stolen technology), the COBRA C.L.A.W.S. can move quickly into position with the latest weapons, to disable any G.I. JOE vehicles that stand in their way. The COBRA C.L.A.W.S. want revenge against HEAVY DUTY because he stopped their plans to take over a global satellite communications network.

WET-SUIT

CODE NAME: WET-SUIT
NAVY SEAL
FILE NAME: FORREST, BRIAN C.
PRIMARY MILITARY SPECIALTY: SEAL
SECONDARY MILITARY SPECIALTY:
UDT (UNDERWATER DEMOLITIONS)
BIRTHPLACE: MYRTLE BEACH, SOUTH CAROLINA
GRADE: E6   **HEIGHT:** 5'11"   **WEIGHT:** 170 lb
SN: 832-5647-LS11

Skill Set	0%	20%	40%	60%	80%	100%
Offense						
Defense						
Vehicle						
Tech						

"Just give me the target and get me under the waves so I can stop those slimy buckets of fish bait!"

WET-SUIT has been called "the nastiest combination of shark, eel, and stingray that you can think of." He was trained as a SEAL, the toughest training in the navy, and is an expert in marine operations and demolitions. When you need someone who can take out a COBRA underwater base with just some fishing line and a knife, he's your guy. In the Atlantis Battle, he stormed COBRA ISLAND and stopped a COBRA MORAY marine assault plan. Because of that, he is now the top target of the COBRA MORAY.

COBRA MORAY

CODE NAME: COBRA MORAY
COBRA UNDERWATER ELITE OPERATIONS
AVERAGE HEIGHT: 5'11"
AVERAGE WEIGHT: 172 lb

Skill Set

	0%	20%	40%	60%	80%	100%
Offense						
Defense						
Vehicle						
Tech						

"Our strength and skills make us the most dominant predators in the ocean."

COBRA MORAY is the code name of the elite underwater forces of COBRA. They are handpicked from the meanest of the COBRA EELS. COBRA MORAYS have been genetically reconstructed to increase their strength and improve their underwater abilities. They have destroyed marine shipping channels, stormed G.I. JOE coastal bases, and caused a lot of misery for anyone who brushes fins with them. WET-SUIT ruined one of their major undersea attacks, and it angers them that an "ordinary guy" could outsmart the COBRA MORAY team.

FROSTBITE™

CODE NAME: FROSTBITE TRANSPORTATION

FILE NAME: SEWARD, FARLEY S.

PRIMARY MILITARY SPECIALTY: ARCTIC SPECIAL OPERATIONS COMMANDER

SECONDARY MILITARY SPECIALTY: VEHICLE SPECIALIST

BIRTHPLACE: GELENA, ALASKA

GRADE: E4   **HEIGHT:** 5'9"   **WEIGHT:** 178 lb

SN: 215-58-9136

Skill Set		0%	20%	40%	60%	80%	100%
	Offense						
	Defense						
	Vehicle						
	Tech						

"The cold north teaches you to always keep your cool, whether you're facing a wall of ice or a wall of NEO-VIPERS."

FROSTBITE was born in a place where summer is a myth and a crowd consists of two people standing on the same acre. He joined the army with the promise of endless challenges. He's an expert in all forms of transportation and can make his way through a blizzard of snow and missiles with a steely eye and a big grin. When the NEO-VIPER team ruined unspoiled tundra by turning it into a bio-weapons compound, FROSTBITE made it his personal duty to put them in the deep freeze, permanently.

NEO-VIPER

CODE NAME: NEO-VIPER

COBRA INFANTRY OFFICERS

AVERAGE HEIGHT: 5'11"

AVERAGE WEIGHT: 190 lb

Skill Set

	0%	20%	40%	60%	80%	100%
Offense						
Defense						
Vehicle						
Tech						

"The G.I. JOE teams are no match for us because they'll be freezing in their tracks while we're doing marathons on the ice."

The NEO-VIPER troops are the next generation of COBRA infantry soldiers. COBRA gave them biotech engineering that regulates their body temperatures so that they are not bothered by extreme cold or heat. They are dropped into COBRA arctic bases to perform environmental sabotage missions and work at COBRA weapons factories. They are the number one enemy of FROSTBITE because they destroyed unspoiled tundra land to set up a bio-weapons research lab.

DUKE

CODE NAME: DUKE
FIRST SERGEANT/G.I. JOE FIELD COMMANDER
FILE NAME: HAUSER, CONRAD S.
PRIMARY MILITARY SPECIALTY: RANGER
SECONDARY MILITARY SPECIALTY:
MILITARY INTELLIGENCE (G2)
BIRTHPLACE: ST. LOUIS, MISSOURI
GRADE: E8 (MASTER SERGEANT)
HEIGHT: 6'1"   WEIGHT: 190 lb
SN: 234-0955-G189

Skill Set	0%	20%	40%	60%	80%	100%
Offense						
Defense						
Vehicle						
Tech						

"I'm out to stop the guy at the top of COBRA because, in the end, he is responsible for all the evil done by his forces."

DUKE is a natural leader, and nobody knows that more than the soldiers he commands. He passed up an officer's commission when he was given the opportunity to handpick the best of the best to form the core of the G.I. JOE team. He believes in leading by example, which is why he's always alongside his troops in the thick of battle. DUKE does not let his feelings come before the mission's goals — but he does take the battle against COBRA COMMANDER personally.

COBRA COMMANDER

CODE NAME: COBRA COMMANDER

SUPREME COBRA LEADER

FILE NAME: CLASSIFIED

PRIMARY MILITARY SPECIALTY: INTELLIGENCE

SECONDARY MILITARY SPECIALTY: ORDNANCE

(EXPERIMENTAL WEAPONRY)

BIRTHPLACE: CLASSIFIED

GRADE: COMMANDER-IN-CHIEF

HEIGHT: 6'0"   WEIGHT: 178 lb

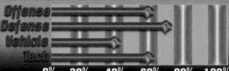

Skill Set	0%	20%	40%	60%	80%	100%
Offense						
Defense						
Vehicle						
Tech						

"COBRA COMMANDER is as cunning and dangerous as the reptile for which he is named."

COBRA COMMANDER is totally ruthless and without a conscience. The leader of the COBRA forces, he wants to take over the world through his COBRA organization and to destroy the G.I. JOE team. He'll do anything to get money and power. He likes to be in the thick of the action when his forces go up against the G.I. JOE team. He hates DUKE, the leader of the G.I. JOE team. He believes that if he can capture DUKE, then all his evil plans will fall into place.

SGT. STALKER™

CODE NAME: SGT. STALKER

EOD (EXPLOSIVE ORDNANCE DISPOSAL)

FILE NAME: WILKINSON, LONZA R.

PRIMARY MILITARY SPECIALTY:

EXPLOSIVE ORDNANCE DISPOSAL

SECONDARY MILITARY SPECIALTY:

MEDIC/INTERPRETER

BIRTHPLACE: DETROIT, MICHIGAN

GRADE: E7   HEIGHT: 6'   WEIGHT: 202 lb

SN: 724-05-LW39

Skill Set	0%	20%	40%	60%	80%	100%
Offense						
Defense						
Vehicle						
Tech						

"You have to be thorough and patient, because one mistake can be deadly."

The U.S. military needs professionals who know how to disarm and destroy explosives. Explosive Ordnance Disposal (EOD) Technicians, like SGT. STALKER, are there to make explosive devices safe. Depending on the kinds of explosives and the situation, SGT. STALKER may blow them up where they are, move them and then blow them up, or disarm them on the spot. Explosive munitions are a favorite of NEO-VIPER COMMANDER, and SGT. STALKER has had to disarm many bombs that were left by NEO-VIPER COMMANDER.

NEO-VIPER COMMANDER ™

CODE NAME: NEO-VIPER COMMANDER
NEO-VIPER LEADER
HEIGHT: 5'10"
WEIGHT: 185 lb

Skill Set

	0%	20%	40%	60%	80%	100%
Offense						
Defense						
Vehicle						
Tech						

"I train my NEO-VIPER troops to be just like me: mean and rotten right down to the soles of their boots."

NEO-VIPER COMMANDER leads the troops that form the back-bone of the COBRA legions. Totally mean, completely obedient, and willing to betray anyone to get ahead, he trains the NEO-VIPER team in all forms of combat and has them ready to deploy on missions at a moment's notice. He thinks that he is superior to the G.I. JOE guys. But SGT. STALKER has ruined many COBRA missions by destroying the bombs before they could explode. The commander now keeps trying to design a device that cannot be defused — even by SGT. STALKER.

17

BIG BEN

CODE NAME: BIG BEN
SAS TROOPER
FILE NAME: BENNET, DAVID J.
PRIMARY MILITARY SPECIALTY: INFANTRY
SECONDARY MILITARY SPECIALTY:
SUBVERSIVE OPERATIONS
BIRTHPLACE: BUFORD, ENGLAND
GRADE: STAFF SERGEANT
HEIGHT: 5'8" WEIGHT: 200 lb

Skill Set	0%	20%	40%	60%	80%	100%
Offense						
Defense						
Vehicle						
Tech						

"I'm here to teach the bad guys that the fight for freedom and justice knows no borders."

The British Special Air Service (SAS) is like the American Special Forces. SAS soldiers work in small units as tightly knit teams. They go behind enemy lines by land, sea, or air for covert missions. Part of the Mobility Troop, BIG BEN has participated in many classified missions. He's now on assignment with the G.I. JOE forces to lend his commando skills to the team. Facing the COBRA ALLEY VIPER forces, BIG BEN showed them why it's never wise to be on the wrong side of an SAS soldier.

COBRA ALLEY VIPER ™

CODE NAME: COBRA ALLEY VIPER
COBRA URBAN ASSAULT TROOPER
AVERAGE HEIGHT: 5'11"
AVERAGE WEIGHT: 170 lb

Skill Set

	0%	20%	40%	60%	80%	100%
Offense						
Defense						
Vehicle						
Tech						

*"We're big, strong, and ruthless!
You don't want to be around when
we come kicking your door down!"*

Recruited from other COBRA divisions, a COBRA ALLEY VIPER goes through extremely tough training in all kinds of urban environments. Only the toughest can successfully jump down thirty feet to a concrete floor while carrying a full combat load — and that's one of the easy exercises. They look and act tough, so people are always running away just at the sight of them. But BIG BEN from the G.I. JOE team did not run — he fought them and sent them packing. Now they live for the day when they can show him that they are the superior fighters.

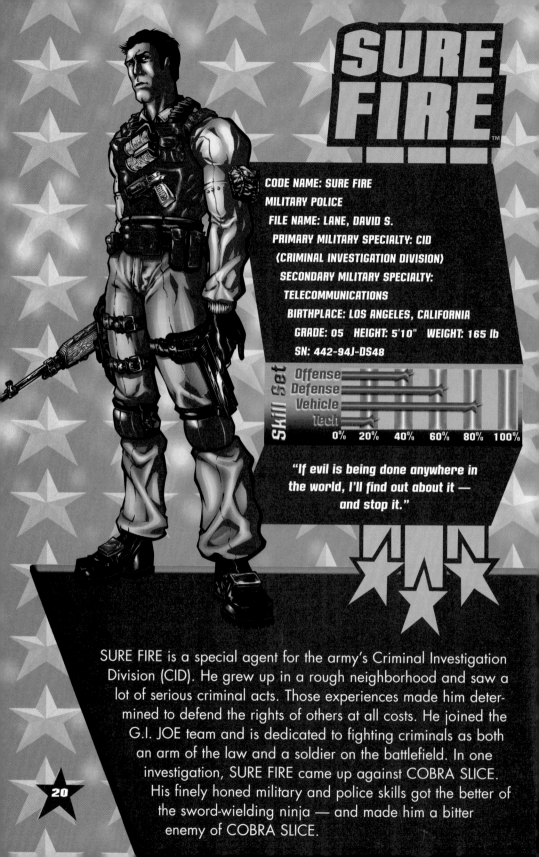

SURE FIRE

CODE NAME: SURE FIRE
MILITARY POLICE
FILE NAME: LANE, DAVID S.
PRIMARY MILITARY SPECIALTY: CID
(CRIMINAL INVESTIGATION DIVISION)
SECONDARY MILITARY SPECIALTY:
TELECOMMUNICATIONS
BIRTHPLACE: LOS ANGELES, CALIFORNIA
GRADE: 05   HEIGHT: 5'10"   WEIGHT: 165 lb
SN: 442-94J-DS48

Skill Set	0%	20%	40%	60%	80%	100%
Offense						
Defense						
Vehicle						
Tech						

"If evil is being done anywhere in the world, I'll find out about it — and stop it."

SURE FIRE is a special agent for the army's Criminal Investigation Division (CID). He grew up in a rough neighborhood and saw a lot of serious criminal acts. Those experiences made him determined to defend the rights of others at all costs. He joined the G.I. JOE team and is dedicated to fighting criminals as both an arm of the law and a soldier on the battlefield. In one investigation, SURE FIRE came up against COBRA SLICE. His finely honed military and police skills got the better of the sword-wielding ninja — and made him a bitter enemy of COBRA SLICE.

COBRA SLICE

CODE NAME: COBRA SLICE

SUPREME COBRA NINJA SWORDSMAN

FILE NAME: CLASSIFIED

PRIMARY MILITARY SPECIALTY: MARTIAL ARTS

SECONDARY MILITARY SPECIALTY:
NINJA SWORD-FIGHTING

BIRTHPLACE: CLASSIFIED

AVERAGE HEIGHT: 5'9"

AVERAGE WEIGHT: 163 lb

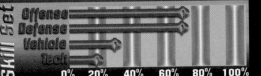

Skill Set

Offense
Defense
Vehicle
Tech

0% 20% 40% 60% 80% 100%

"I fear no mortal man in face-to-face combat, but my sword cuts easiest from behind."

Captured COBRA documents indicate that COBRA SLICE may be a renegade ninja from the same clan as STORM SHADOW. It is believed that COBRA SLICE created his own evil sword technique by observing the battle strategies of scorpions and adapting the movements into a backhand sword-slash that he calls the "Scorpion Slash." COBRA SLICE was humiliated when he fought SURE FIRE from the G.I. JOE team — and lost. He lives for the day when he'll meet SURE FIRE again, and this time he'll teach him a lesson he won't forget.

MIRAGE

CODE NAME: MIRAGE
WEAPONS EXPERT
FILE NAME: BAIKUN, JOSEPH R.
PRIMARY MILITARY SPECIALTY:
  ROCKET FIRE ASSAULT
  SECONDARY MILITARY SPECIALTY: HEAVY ARTILLERY
  BIRTHPLACE: MOLSEN, WASHINGTON
  GRADE: E6   HEIGHT: 5'11"   WEIGHT: 185 lb
  SN: 606-JB-824

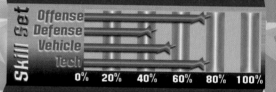

Skill Set		0%	20%	40%	60%	80%	100%
Offense							
Defense							
Vehicle							
Tech							

"If evil is being done anywhere in the world, I'll find out about it — and stop it."

Fighting the evil COBRA organization calls for powerful weapons and skilled soldiers trained to use them. MIRAGE is just such a soldier. He's a specialist in weapons, from machine guns to the TOW missile systems. MIRAGE advises and trains the G.I. JOE team on what to use and when to use it. He takes particular delight in going up against the COBRA VIPER forces, who have lots of weaponry but don't know the best way to use it. MIRAGE showed them that all the firepower in the world will never beat a team of skilled soldiers.

COBRA VIPER

CODE NAME: COBRA VIPER

COBRA INFANTRYMAN

AVERAGE HEIGHT: 5'10"

AVERAGE WEIGHT: 177 lb

Skill Set

	0%	20%	40%	60%	80%	100%
Offense						
Defense						
Vehicle						
Tech						

"G.I. JOE be warned! We have more weapons and more guts than you could ever hope to have."

The COBRA VIPER force is made up of the grunts from the COBRA legions. If there's a dirty job that needs doing, these guys are first in line. They wear multilayered body armor and wraparound helmets with built-in radio telecommunications gear, and carry multi-burst laser pistols, commando rifles, and grenade launchers. They're ready at a moment's notice to cause harm and do damage anywhere that COBRA COMMANDER sends them. When MIRAGE defeated them despite their massive weaponry, the COBRA VIPER team vowed revenge.

GENERAL TOMAHAWK ™

CODE NAME: GENERAL TOMAHAWK

G.I. JOE COMMANDER

FILE NAME: ABERNATHY, CLAYTON M.

BIRTHPLACE: DENVER, COLORADO

GRADE: O8 (MAJOR GENERAL)

HEIGHT: 6'1"   WEIGHT: 190 lb

SN: RA2-127-5406

Skill Set	0%	20%	40%	60%	80%	100%
Offense						
Defense						
Vehicle						
Tech						

"The commander of any team must be an example to his troops in courage, dedication, and skill."

When GENERAL TOMAHAWK orders his men into battle, he leads the attack. He believes that a general should be with his troops to show them how to fight and how to win. A West Point graduate and two-star general, he has been in plenty of conflicts around the world. The United States Army relies on soldiers like GENERAL TOMAHAWK to carry on the proud, tough tradition of America's fighting forces. He has been after the HEADMAN for some time. He wants to stop the dangerous smuggler and thief who has threatened the peace of many nations.

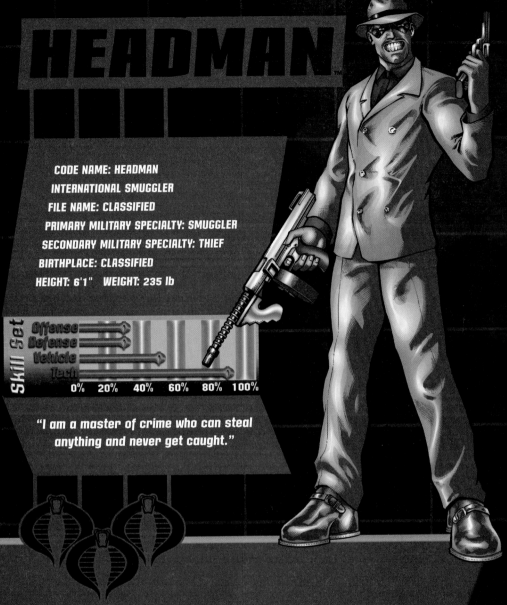

HEADMAN™

CODE NAME: HEADMAN

INTERNATIONAL SMUGGLER

FILE NAME: CLASSIFIED

PRIMARY MILITARY SPECIALTY: SMUGGLER

SECONDARY MILITARY SPECIALTY: THIEF

BIRTHPLACE: CLASSIFIED

HEIGHT: 6'1"   WEIGHT: 235 lb

Skill Set

Offense

Defense

Vehicle

Tech

0%   20%   40%   60%   80%   100%

"I am a master of crime who can steal anything and never get caught."

HEADMAN started out robbing convenience stores and soon learned the ropes of high-end crime while serving time in prison. A hardened criminal, HEADMAN doesn't think twice about hurting anyone who gets in the way of his plans. He steals anything for the right price — government secrets, weapon system specifications, and priceless art treasures. His thefts have undermined the safety of countries. He has managed to escape GENERAL TOMAHAWK time and again. But HEADMAN wants to put an end to the tough general, once and for all.

AGENT SCARLETT™

CODE NAME: AGENT SCARLETT
COUNTERINTELLIGENCE AGENT
FILE NAME: O'HARA, SHANA M.
PRIMARY MILITARY SPECIALTY: COUNTERINTELLIGENCE
SECONDARY MILITARY SPECIALTY: CLASSIFIED
BIRTHPLACE: ATLANTA, GEORGIA
GRADE: E5   HEIGHT: 5'7"   WEIGHT: 120 lb
SN: RA24-29-7634

Skill Set	0%	20%	40%	60%	80%	100%
Offense						
Defense						
Vehicle						
Tech						

"People ask me what it takes to be a good agent. I say: integrity, courage, and intelligence."

The U.S. military relies on special agents to gather information about the plans of its enemies. One of these agents is AGENT SCARLETT. She started her counterintelligence work by analyzing evidence, setting up surveillance equipment, and preparing reports. After she proved her abilities in small missions, she began to conduct field operations. On one secret operation, she encountered ZARTAN, a master of disguise who impersonated a G.I. JOE team member. Now AGENT SCARLETT vows to unmask ZARTAN so that he can never endanger anyone again.

ZARTAN

CODE NAME: ZARTAN

MASTER OF DISGUISE

FILE NAME: UNKNOWN

PRIMARY MILITARY SPECIALTY: DISGUISE

BIRTHPLACE: UNKNOWN

HEIGHT: 5'10"   WEIGHT: 176 lb

Skill Set

	0%	20%	40%	60%	80%	
Offense						
Defense						
Vehicle						
Tech						

"I can be anyone, anywhere. You will never know that you are talking to me, unless I wish it."

ZARTAN can become anyone by changing his looks, personality, and voice. He's a genius with makeup and disguises and speaks over twenty languages and dialects. He can get in and out of places the size of a shoe box. He was forced to abandon a deadly mission when AGENT SCARLETT saw through one of his disguises. This was the first time someone had uncovered any of his deceptions, so now he lives to put her away. A mysterious member of COBRA, he proved his value to the organization by impersonating COBRA COMMANDER. He then revealed his disguise to the stunned — and impressed — commander.

DUSTY™

CODE NAME: DUSTY
DESERT TROOPER
FILE NAME: TADUR, RONALD W.
PRIMARY MILITARY SPECIALTY: INFANTRY
SECONDARY MILITARY SPECIALTY:
REFRIGERATION AND AIR-CONDITIONING
MAINTENANCE
BIRTHPLACE: LAS VEGAS, NEVADA
GRADE: E4   HEIGHT: 6'1"   WEIGHT: 220 lb
SN: 371-11-RT05

Skill Set

	0%	20%	40%	60%	80%	100%
Offense						
Defense						
Vehicle						
Tech						

"Training to be a soldier is the toughest task you'll ever take on, but it's also the greatest."

The U.S. Army must be equipped to fight for American values in any climate. To do that, they have trained a special breed of soldier: desert infantry soldiers. These brave individuals train in the harshest conditions. DUSTY is no stranger to danger in the desert — snakes, scorpions, dust storms, and the temperature extremes. These conditions only strengthen his determination to hunt down and defeat the evil forces of COBRA. And DUSTY loves turning up the heat on DESERT COBRA C.L.A.W.S.!

DESERT COBRA C.L.A.W.S.

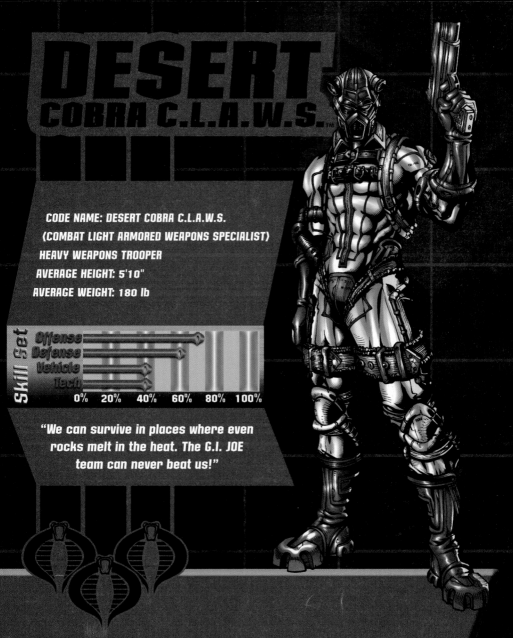

CODE NAME: DESERT COBRA C.L.A.W.S.
(COMBAT LIGHT ARMORED WEAPONS SPECIALIST)
HEAVY WEAPONS TROOPER
AVERAGE HEIGHT: 5'10"
AVERAGE WEIGHT: 180 lb

Skill Set

	0%	20%	40%	60%	80%	100%
Offense						
Defense						
Vehicle						
Tech						

"We can survive in places where even rocks melt in the heat. The G.I. JOE team can never beat us!"

DESERT COBRA C.L.A.W.S. take a lot of punishment and dish out even more. The DESERT COBRA C.L.A.W.S. have technology to help them survive in the hottest, driest regions of the world — special suits with heat-deflection insulation and a body-cooling system. That means they can hide out where no one will find them, until it's time to strike. But they can't hide from G.I. JOE team member DUSTY. He's tracked down their remote, hidden camps and crushed their evil plans. He's their number one enemy.

29

BEACHHEAD™

CODE NAME: BEACHHEAD
AMPHIBIOUS AND AIRBORNE ASSAULT TROOPER
FILE NAME: SNEEDEN, WAYNE R.
PRIMARY MILITARY SPECIALTY: INFANTRY
SECONDARY MILITARY SPECIALTY:
SMALL ARMS ARMORER
BIRTHPLACE: AUBURN, ALABAMA
GRADE: E7 HEIGHT: 6' WEIGHT: 182 lb
SN: 902-46-SW14

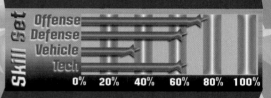

Skill Set

	0%	20%	40%	60%	80%	100%
Offense						
Defense						
Vehicle						
Tech						

"Getting angry is a total waste of time and energy. I'd rather get the job done!"

A former Ranger School instructor, BEACHHEAD is a qualified expert with all NATO and former Warsaw Pact small arms. He likes to be the first one out of the helicopter on a combat assault because he knows that he can provide defense against enemy fire so the rest of his team can deploy safely. A self-reliant, can-do person with a healthy self-esteem, BEACHHEAD is the natural adversary of DR. MINDBENDER, the COBRA master of mind control.

DR. MINDBENDER

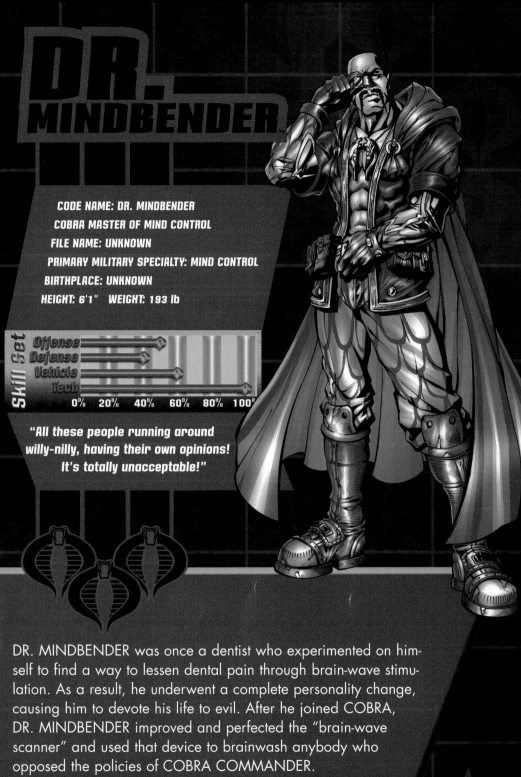

CODE NAME: DR. MINDBENDER

COBRA MASTER OF MIND CONTROL

FILE NAME: UNKNOWN

PRIMARY MILITARY SPECIALTY: MIND CONTROL

BIRTHPLACE: UNKNOWN

HEIGHT: 6'1"   WEIGHT: 193 lb

Skill Set

	0%	20%	40%	60%	80%	100%
Offense						
Defense						
Vehicle						
Tech						

"All these people running around willy-nilly, having their own opinions! It's totally unacceptable!"

DR. MINDBENDER was once a dentist who experimented on himself to find a way to lessen dental pain through brain-wave stimulation. As a result, he underwent a complete personality change, causing him to devote his life to evil. After he joined COBRA, DR. MINDBENDER improved and perfected the "brain-wave scanner" and used that device to brainwash anybody who opposed the policies of COBRA COMMANDER. Independent thinkers with strong personalities annoy DR. MINDBENDER. He has had a long-standing personal antagonism toward BEACHHEAD.

BLOWTORCH ™

CODE NAME: BLOWTORCH
FLAMETHROWER
FILE NAME: HANRAHAN, TIMOTHY P.
PRIMARY MILITARY SPECIALTY: INFANTRY
SPECIAL WEAPONS
SECONDARY MILITARY SPECIALTY: COMBAT
ENGINEER
BIRTHPLACE: TAMPA, FLORIDA
GRADE: E6 HEIGHT: 6' WEIGHT: 187 lb
SN: 527-34-RA09

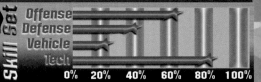

Skill Set	0%	20%	40%	60%	80%	100%
Offense						
Defense						
Vehicle						
Tech						

"Fire is supposed to be our friend, but when we get careless with it, we find out just how ferocious an enemy it can be."

BLOWTORCH is a qualified expert with flamethrowers, pyrotechnics, and heat-projection devices. Harsh arctic weather conditions reduce the effectiveness of flame weapons, which is why BLOWTORCH has a bone to pick with COBRA SNOW SERPENT forces. But BLOWTORCH is all about fire safety. He'd much rather see a flame extinguished than ignited. Why would somebody who thinks like that want to work with flame weapons? Because he wants the fire to be under control, and he thinks he's the best one to do it.

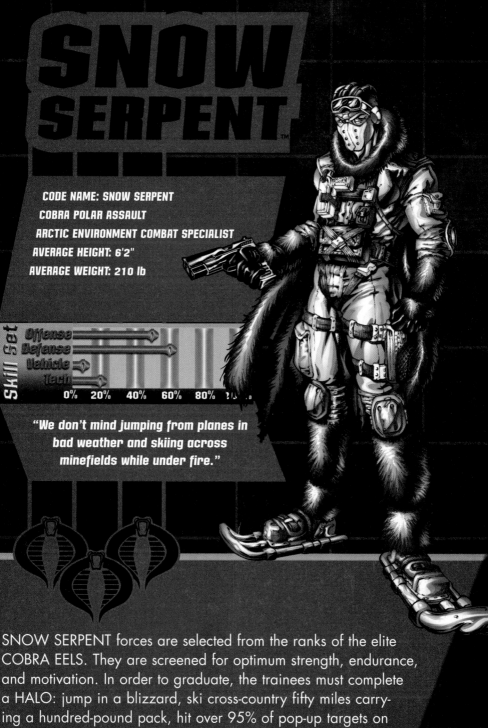

SNOW SERPENT ™

CODE NAME: SNOW SERPENT
COBRA POLAR ASSAULT
ARCTIC ENVIRONMENT COMBAT SPECIALIST
AVERAGE HEIGHT: 6'2"
AVERAGE WEIGHT: 210 lb

Skill Set

	0%	20%	40%	60%	80%	100%
Offense						
Defense						
Vehicle						
Tech						

"We don't mind jumping from planes in bad weather and skiing across minefields while under fire."

SNOW SERPENT forces are selected from the ranks of the elite COBRA EELS. They are screened for optimum strength, endurance, and motivation. In order to graduate, the trainees must complete a HALO: jump in a blizzard, ski cross-country fifty miles carrying a hundred-pound pack, hit over 95% of pop-up targets on the combat range, and swim a hundred meters in freezing water while carrying fifty pounds of ammunition. Flame weapons can really ruin the day of a SNOW SERPENT. This is why they have a picture of BLOWTORCH on a dartboard at COBRA headquarters.

FLINT

CODE NAME: FLINT
FILE NAME: FAIRBORNE, DASHIELL R.
PRIMARY MILITARY SPECIALTY: INFANTRY
SECONDARY MILITARY SPECIALTY: ROTARY WING
AIRCRAFT PILOT
BIRTHPLACE: WICHITA, KANSAS
GRADE: WO2 HEIGHT: 5'10" WEIGHT: 185 lb
SN: 307-62-FD87

Skill Set
Offense
Defense
Vehicle
Tech

0% 20% 40% 60% 80% 100%

"We're not heroes, we're just
doing our job."

As a graduate of the Special Forces School and Flight Warrant Officers School, FLINT brings a broad intellectual background as well as technical skills and tactical knowledge to the G.I. JOE team. FLINT is believed to have led many secret hostage rescue missions in dangerous areas. It doesn't bother FLINT in the least that he will never receive credit for these missions. FLINT finds the BARONESS especially despicable because of her intelligence and educational background. He thinks that she should simply know better.

BARONESS

CODE NAME: BARONESS
DIRECTOR OF INTELLIGENCE FOR COBRA COMMAND
COBRA INTELLIGENCE OFFICER
FILE NAME: CLASSIFIED
ALIAS: ANISTASIA DeCOBRAY
BIRTHPLACE: CLASSIFIED
HEIGHT: 5'5"   WEIGHT: 110 lb

Skill Set
Offense
Defense
Vehicle
Tech
0%   20%   40%   60%   80%   100%

"The ideals of COBRA are the true
reflection of the masses that
comprise the Me Generation."

Born into wealth, the BARONESS involved herself with dangerous
groups before aligning herself with COBRA. She has wormed
her way into the confidences of both COBRA COMMANDER and
DESTRO. As the Director of Intelligence for COBRA COMMAND,
she conducts many evil operations for COBRA. She has an
intense hatred of the G.I. JOE team and especially of FLINT,
because she's jealous of intelligence, strength, and courage.

DIAL TONE

CODE NAME: DIAL TONE
COMMUNICATIONS EXPERT
FILE NAME: MORELLI, JACK S.
PRIMARY MILITARY SPECIALTY: RADIO
TELECOMMUNICATIONS
SECONDARY MILITARY SPECIALTY: INFANTRY
BIRTHPLACE: EUGENE, OREGON
GRADE: E6   HEIGHT: 5'9"   WEIGHT: 165 lb
SN: 858-9142-92KH

Skill Set	0%	20%	40%	60%	80%	100%
Offense						
Defense						
Vehicle						
Tech						

"I make sure my message gets out loud and clear."

DIAL TONE served as a telecommunications expert for years before volunteering for duty with the G.I. JOE team. He can tune in on enemy transmitter frequencies and locate their coordinates, then attack with pinpoint accuracy. An expert electronics repairman, he also holds the record for setting up a mobile satellite transmitter under battlefield conditions in less than three minutes. His main responsibility is to stay in touch with headquarters and get the team to the correct pickup site. Nothing stops him from doing his job — he even finds ways to get his team out when there is no radio contact.

FAST BLAST VIPER ™

CODE NAME: FAST BLAST VIPER

BRANCH FIELD COMMANDER

SPECIAL TRAINING: HAND-TO-HAND COMBAT,
FIELD WEAPONS, MARTIAL ARTS, DEMOLITIONS

AVERAGE HEIGHT: 5'10"

AVERAGE WEIGHT: 185 lb

Skill Set

	0%	20%	40%	60%	80%	100%
Offense						
Defense						
Vehicle						
Tech						

"We fight until we win."

Armed with specially designed battlefield weapons, FAST BLAST VIPER forces are sent out to lead an attack with only one objective: stop G.I. JOE forces. Each one has learned to withstand tough battlefield conditions. To make them more formidable, FAST BLAST VIPER members have been trained to wipe out any fear or hesitation in attack situations — they show no emotion, no matter what happens. They are mean and aggressive opponents with many combat skills and are tough enemies of the G.I. JOE team.

TUNNEL RAT ™

CODE NAME: TUNNEL RAT
ARMY RANGER
FILE NAME: LEE, NICKY
PRIMARY MILITARY SPECIALTY: E.O.D.
(EXPLOSIVE ORDNANCE DISPOSAL)
SECONDARY MILITARY SPECIALTY: COMBAT
ENGINEER
BIRTHPLACE: BROOKLYN, NEW YORK
GRADE: E5   HEIGHT: 5'8"   WEIGHT: 153 lb
SN: 367-84-NL90

Skill Set	0%	20%	40%	60%	80%	100%
Offense						
Defense						
Vehicle						
Tech						

"A Ranger doesn't let anything get in the way of accomplishing his mission."

TUNNEL RAT earned his code name through his daring missions into dark, narrow tunnels. He goes into the tunnels to gather information or to sabotage the hidden areas. TUNNEL RAT is one of the Army Rangers, the elite soldiers who are sent on secret, highly dangerous missions. Only the best are able to complete the tough physical and leadership exercises that make sure Rangers always move fast, strike hard, and never quit. And those who do are men like TUNNEL RAT — exceptionally brave, highly skilled soldiers in one of America's finest fighting forces.

UNDERTOW

CODE NAME: UNDERTOW
COBRA FROGMAN
AVERAGE HEIGHT: 5'10"
AVERAGE WEIGHT: 177 lb

Skill Set	0%	20%	40%	60%	80%	100%
Offense						
Defense						
Vehicle						
Tech						

"We swim through anything to get the job done."

Any frogman can operate efficiently in clean water, under optimum conditions, but the UNDERTOW are specially trained to function and fight in the murky, polluted waters surrounding busy industrial and military waterfronts. Their wet suits are made of a nontoxic, anticorrosive material, and their face masks are coated with silicone to repel oil slicks. They are almost impossible to capture or defeat because others cannot enter the hostile water environments in which they work.

NUNCHUK ®

CODE NAME: NUNCHUK
MARTIAL ARTS EXPERT
FILE NAME: BALDUCCI, RALPH
PRIMARY MILITARY SPECIALTY: SELF-DEFENSE
INSTRUCTOR
SECONDARY MILITARY SPECIALTY: ORDNANCE
BIRTHPLACE: BROOKLYN, NEW YORK
GRADE: E5   HEIGHT: 5'11"   WEIGHT: 175 lb
SN: 980-4290-KB22

Skill	0%	20%	40%	60%	80%	100%
Offense						
Defense						
Vehicle						
Tech						

"Speed, power, and agility —
those are the skills, but they
must be used with wisdom."

NUNCHUK has prepared the G.I. JOE team to defend itself
against enemies who may use the martial arts in close combat.
NUNCHUK is an expert in most forms of martial arts and incor-
porates key moves into the traditional fighting techniques of
the American soldier. During a mission to stop a sabotage
attempt against a nuclear facility, NUNCHUK fought
against FIREFLY, a martial arts master so skilled that
NUNCHUK barely escaped with his life. Now he's out to
get FIREFLY, furious that someone would use the martial
arts for evil purposes.

FIREFLY

CODE NAME: FIREFLY

COBRA SABOTEUR

FILE NAME: CLASSIFIED

PRIMARY MILITARY SPECIALTY: SABOTAGE

BIRTHPLACE: CLASSIFIED

HEIGHT: 5'9"   WEIGHT: 170 lb

Skill Set

Offense

Defense

Vehicle

Tech

0%   20%   40%   60%   80%   100%

"COBRA calls me in to do the impossible, because I can make it happen."

FIREFLY uses his skills to break into places that are supposed to be out of reach. He can scale a cliff or building as easily as a fly walking up a wall. He has highly developed reflexes and expertise in hand-to-hand martial arts combat. COBRA likes to use him when a single saboteur is needed to quietly break into a secured location and cause some trouble. He encountered the martial arts master NUNCHUK and, for the first time, had to escape before being captured. Now he wants revenge for his humiliating defeat.

41

BRAWLER

ARMORED TROOP TRANSPORT

WEIGHT: 2.7 tons
SPEED: (with 4-man crew, fully loaded) 85 mph
off-road, 4-wheel drive: 45 mph
RANGE: 420 miles (fully loaded)

ORDNANCE:
★ 2x side-mounted .50 cal assault machine guns w/500 rounds each
★ 2x rear triple-threat rocket pods
★ 6-shot bunker blaster missile launcher

COBRA HISS IV™

ARMORED PERSONNEL CARRIER

WEIGHT: 11.25 tons
SPEED: 75 mph
RANGE: 275 miles (fully loaded)

ARMAMENT:

* ★ dorsal-mounted dual fed .50 cal armor-piercing assault cannon and .30 cal machine gun, each w/750 rounds
* ★ side-mounted portable pulse cannon w/rechargeable power cell
* ★ 2x hiss rockets
* ★ 1 side-mounted burst pod w/7 rockets

ROAD REBEL ™

ONE-MAN SELF-PROPELLED CANNON

WEIGHT: 7 tons
SPEED: 47 mph
RANGE: 126 miles (fully loaded)

ARMAMENT:
★ 90 mm antitank cannon w/20 rounds
★ portable flamethrower w/2 hours worth of fuel

COBRA VENOM CYCLE

RAPID-FIRE MOTORCYCLE

WEIGHT: 390 lb (motorcycle); 486 lb (gunner sidecar)
SPEED: 110 mph (2-man crew, fully loaded)
RANGE: 360 miles (fully loaded)

ARMAMENT:

★ sidecar-mounted coils rocket launcher w/4 rounds
★ 70 mm sidecar-mounted plasma cannon

NIGHT ATTACK CHOPPER™

ARMORED GUNSHIP

WEIGHT: 14.5 tons
SPEED: 175 mph (5-man crew, fully loaded)
RANGE: 345 miles (fully loaded)

ORDNANCE:
* ★ Fast-drop winch
* ★ Laser-guided target designator

ARMAMENT:
* ★ 2x wing-mounted rotary field sweeper antipersonnel rocket
* ★ pods nose-mounted 30 mm antitank mini-gun w/2,000 rounds
* ★ 2x nose-mounted .50 cal machine guns, 1,200 rounds each
* ★ portable Vulcan mini-gun w/750 rounds
* ★ portable pulse cannon w/20 rounds
* ★ 2x 150-pound canard wing-mounted general-purpose
  demolition bombs

DESTRO'S DOMINATOR

HOVER TANK

WEIGHT: 11,000 lb
SPEED: Land: 65 mph road, 42 cross-country; Air: 120 mph
RANGE: Land: 325 miles; Air: 410 miles (fully loaded)

ARMAMENT:
★ 4x scorpion missiles
★ 2x dual-mounted .50 cal laser cannons w/200-round power cell each
★ side-mounted armor-piercing Gatling gun w/1,000-round drum

SAND RAZOR™

DESERT SURVEILLANCE VEHICLE

WEIGHT: 2.25 tons
SPEED: (3-man crew, fully loaded) 95 mph (off-road);
52 mph (4-wheel drive)
RANGE: 335 miles (fully loaded)

ORDNANCE:
★ portable M-60 machine gun w/200 rounds
★ triple-barrel mini-gun w/700 rounds
★ 4x pulse mine sweeper guns
★ 2x 122 mm antitank cannons w/6 rounds each
★ 3x surface-to-surface computer- or laser-designated
targeted high-explosive or incendiary missiles